apples and pumpkins

BY ANNE ROCKWELL   ILLUSTRATED BY LIZZY ROCKWELL

ALADDIN · New York · London · Toronto · Sydney · New Delhi

For Lucrezia and Ludovica

ALADDIN

An imprint of Simon & Schuster Children's Publishing Division

1230 Avenue of the Americas, New York, NY 10020

This Aladdin paperback edition September 2012

For information about special discounts for bulk purchases, please contact

Simon & Schuster Special Sales at 1-866-506-1949 or business@simonandschuster.com.

The Simon & Schuster Speakers Bureau can bring authors to your live event.

For more information or to book an event contact the Simon & Schuster Speakers

Bureau at 1-866-248-3049 or visit our website at www.simonspeakers.com.

Designed by Jessica Handelman

The text of this book was set in Kindergarten.

The illustrations for this book were rendered in watercolor and pencil.

Manufactured in China

0215 SCP

10 9 8 7 6

The Library of Congress has cataloged the hardcover edition as follows:

Rockwell, Anne F.

Apples and pumpkins / by Anne Rockwell ; illustrated by Lizzy

Rockwell. — 1st Aladdin hardcover ed.

p. cm.

Summary: In preparation for Halloween night, a family visits

Mr. Comstock's farm to pick apples and pumpkins.

ISBN 978-1-4424-0350-5 (hardcover)

[1. Autumn—Fiction. 2. Halloween—Fiction. 3. Apples—Fiction.

4. Pumpkin—Fiction.] I. Rockwell, Lizzy, ill. II. Title.

PZ7.R5943Ap 2011

[E]—dc22

2009035317

ISBN 978-1-4424-7656-1 (paperback)

When red and yellow leaves are on the trees,

we go to the Comstock Farm

to pick apples and pumpkins.

Mr. Comstock gives us a bushel basket to put our apples in.

Geese and chickens and a big, fat turkey walk with us on our way to the orchard, where the apples grow.

My father picks apples.
My mother does too.

I climb into a little apple tree
and pick the reddest apples of all.

When our basket is full
of red and shiny apples,

we go to the field
where the pumpkins grow.

I look and look until I find
the best pumpkin of them all.

My father cuts it from the vine.

I carry it back
to the car.

At home we carve
a jack-o'-lantern face
on our big, orange pumpkin.

We put a candle inside and
light it. Now our pumpkin
looks scary and funny, too.

On Halloween night we
put our pumpkin on the doorstep.
My mother gives away lots of
our red and shiny apples
for trick-or-treat,

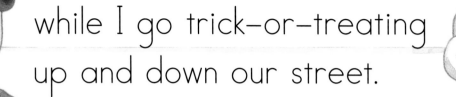

while I go trick-or-treating
up and down our street.